WULFGAR AND THE DRAGON

WULFGAR AND THE DRAGON

Christina Eastwood

Christian Year Publications

ISBN-13: 978 1 872734 78 1

Typeset by John Ritchie Ltd., Kilmarnock
Printed by Bell & Bain Ltd., Glasgow

Contents

Foreword

I really enjoyed this short story, a worthy second instalment of *Wulfgar the Saxon*. As with the first book, this is a veritable history-tale whose authentic names and places help create the Saxon 'feel'. As well as the drama and excitement of dragon encounters, there are reflective and poignant moments too. I especially appreciate how the author has cleverly woven spiritual lessons into the narrative. My interest was piqued quickly and maintained until the end - perhaps we can hope for further Wulfgar adventures to come!

Philip Bell

CEO of Creation Ministries International UK
and author of *Evolution and the Christian Faith*

DEDICATION

To my newest loved ones
Hugh Jones and Grace Eastwood

ACKNOWLEDGEMENTS

My grateful thanks are due to my husband whose enthusiasm and encouragement got the job done when I might have given up.

Introduction

"Wulfgar and the *Dragon?*" I hear you say, "What is this? Surely dragons are mythical beasts!" Well, it has to be said that opinions differ on that point.[1] The Anglo-Saxon Chronicle mentions dragons and there is another word beginning with d that describes reptile-like beasts that everyone knows were real because we can still find their bones. I am definitely not the only person to be convinced they were around more recently than some people might tell you! It would certainly explain why you can read tales about dragons told by people all over the world – not to mention that some of those bones have been found to contain soft tissue and red blood cells[2] so they are not so *very* old after all ... If you still can't guess what I'm talking about I'm not giving the game away – you'll have to read the story.

---

[1] https://creation.com/images/pds/tj/j24_1/j24_1_32-34.pdf
[2] Schweitzer, M.H., *et al.*, Analyses of soft tissue from *Tyrannosaurus rex* suggest the presence of protein, Science 316(5822):277-280, 2007

Chapter One
Hund

This is the account of Wulfgar the carpenter, son of Waelwulf, descendant of Woden, son of Sceaf, son of Noah, the flood-borne, who desires to put on record events of the years of our Lord eight hundred and seventy eight and eight hundred and eighty so that whoever reads may know the goodness of God to his creatures, the nobility of our King Alfred, the bravery (God giving them strength) of the men of the village of Leofham, the courage of our Thane Pelhere and the wisdom of Morcant the Celt, a record of which I have made also in another place.[3] I begin my account in April, the eight month, as some of our chroniclers count it, of the first year named above.

It was only thanks to Morcant the Celt's special pleading that the dog was not drowned with the rest of the hideous puppies that formed the wolfhound's litter. Thane Pelhere had been proud of the pair of massive Irish hunting dogs the king had given him. Only the most favoured of King Alfred's men received such a mark of royal gratitude. He was delighted when he understood that the bitch was about to produce a litter of puppies. When the puppies arrived, however, it was immediately obvious that something had gone wrong. From birth they were anything but royal and looked nothing like their wolfhound mother. They were not going to be of any use as dignified symbols that would enhance the thane's noble status nor could they be given away as marks of his special favour. Disgusted, he ordered them to be disposed of.

---

[3]See *Wulfgar the Saxon*

"Can't she just keep one, my Thane?" asked the little Celt as we both attended on the thane in his hall. "It is cruel to take them all from her."

"You are too soft hearted, Morcant," replied the thane, "but if you want one of the ugly things, help yourself."

"A righteous man takes care of his animals, my Thane," said Morcant quietly but the thane seemed preoccupied and only grunted, more important worries now filled his mind.

"I will have to supply more men to the king for his defence-building work, Morcant," he said. "It is going to be hard to spare them."

"Indeed!" said Morcant, stooping down to examine the sleeping puppies. "We are going to be stretched. The king's plans are wise, however, and no time can be lost in carrying them out."

"If the king succeeds in building up all the old fortified towns and strongholds, in time he will cover Wessex with a network of strong forts well laid out and capable of being garrisoned at a moment's notice. Then, we will at last be secure from Viking attack," agreed the thane. "Almost any sacrifice would be worth making for that. With that security we can prosper. Without it we are always at the mercy of the Vikings. I don't trust that Viking leader, Guthram, baptised or not! Suppose he goes back on his word? They've done that before, you know. If an army of his fellow Vikings arrive from overseas is he really going to fight *against* them? I don't think so! No, he will invite them into the Danelaw where he rules and that will give them a base to work from. Then it will be the same old story: raids, destruction, war and Wessex in peril again. The king is right. We will have to strain every nerve to ensure we can defend ourselves and we must do it *now* while we have a respite."

"Have you seen the king's plans for extending the fortifications?" asked Morcant.

"Only in the most general way," replied the thane. "He is concentrating on crossroads to make it easier for the fyrdmen that form his army to reach them – and merchants too so that trade can be made easier when the Vikings have been banished for ever. The king's plans are practical, I understand, streets laid out straight and criss-crossed, good access for the fyrdmen and so on."

"This of itself will bring prosperity to Wessex," remarked Morcant thoughtfully.

"I don't know about that," said the thane, a little grumpy now. "What I want to know is how we keep going here in Leofham in the short term. By the time we've supplied men, extra food rents, not to mention *church scot* to the monks, we are going to be hard pressed to have enough to survive. This year we will be quite well provided for if all goes well although it will be a bit hard in July for some families. But we have to try to look to the future. We must get the maximum sown and harrowed now and the minimum lost if we can. I'm glad the ploughing of the farrow is well under way and they have started sowing the barley and rye now."

Morcant nodded, "Eanflæde and I will do all we can to help, my thane," he said.

The thane was aghast, "No, no, no," he said quickly, "not you. You are the king's spiritual advisor and in any case we need you to copy out the holy books that were found on the Viking ship. You are a bit of an irregular it is true, Morcant, but King Alfred has made it quite plain that, as he understands it, Wessex needs three classes of people: the soldiers to fight to protect the kingdom, workers to grow the food needed, and clerics to pray. You may be a married man and outside the regular system of the church, but you are definitely in the last of those groups and the king would be horrified if you were taken from your holy labours to drive the plough."

When the village had acquired a set of books forming the Word of God from the loot found in a Viking longship, Morcant had been tasked with the job of copying and translating it into Anglo Saxon by the king himself.[4]

"We must all of us pray," he said quietly.

"True, true," said the thane and turned to me.

"Wulfgar, if the king calls for *you* I will send you," he said. "A skilled carpenter would be useful to him in his grand building endeavours."

And with that we were dismissed.

Some weeks later a lad with a message arrived outside my workshop hut.

"Ho, Wulfgar," he called, "the thane sent this to Master Morcant but when I took it round to him he said it was for Swefred – is he with you?"

Young Swefred, son of Eanflæde and stepson of Morcant,[5] was my helper now, trying to learn the craft as I myself had done from my own master, Beorthelm. Together we were repairing a cart that had seen better days. Swefred crawled out from under it and the lad pulled something wrapped in a rag from inside his jerkin. He handed the bundle to Swefred who gasped with pleasure.

"O! it's the puppy!" he said in delight. "It's big enough to leave its mother at last! Master Morcant said I could have it for my own so long as I trained it well."

The little thing wriggled and struggled in his arms, trying to lick his face. It was easy to see that, although the wolfhound was its mother, its father must have been a completely different kind of animal. Its legs were short and stubby and its tail minute. All it

---

[4]*See Wulfgar and the Vikings*
[5]*See Wulfgar and the Vikings*

seemed to have inherited from its mother was the beginnings of a shaggy coat and clear bright eyes. Swefred set it down on the ground on its fat little legs and it capered round him joyfully.

"Oh, he is a funny little thing!" exclaimed Swefred in delight. "How could anyone think of drowning him?"

"What will you call him?" I asked.

"Just Hund, I think," said Swefred. "Short and easy for him to remember."

"Well, get him some water to drink, a few rags to make a bed and then tie him up somewhere," I said. "We have work to do here."

In May everyone in Leofham is kept working at full stretch. We were already short-handed through the King's great building projects and so the ploughing of the fallow was still not finished. Spring crops were being sown and in the village gardens cabbages, onions, leeks and garlic were all requiring attention to say nothing of herbs and the flax and dye plants we needed for clothing. Our cows were in full milk and so there were cheeses to be made and the round of hedging, ditching and general repairs to buildings and tools never let up for a moment – the latter keeping me particularly busy. Even so, Swefred found time somehow to train Hund and care for him. You never saw him about the village now without the little dog at his heels.

But although Hund's behaviour soon became exemplary, his appearance did not improve with age. I don't know if you can imagine a huge, graceful wolfhound shorn of its elegant long limbs and somehow perched on legs belonging to a much less dignified animal, but poor Hund could not be described in any other way. A wolfhound is swift, brave and loyal. Although Hund was certainly loyal and perhaps would be brave when it came to the test, anyone could see he was not built for speed.

When Swefred did duty with the other children defending

the new sown crops from birds, Hund went with him. Swefred trained Hund to stay by him quietly until freed from this irksome duty by a word of command. Gradually Hund became capable of sitting immobile as a carving of a dog for long stretches of time. As pressure on our menfolk mounted that year I had to release Swefred more and more often for work on the land while I struggled on alone in the workshop. He and Hund were completely inseparable and Swefred began to train him to help with the animals, rounding up sheep or herding cows. The dog grew and learned quickly and Swefred had the knack of training him. A short whistle would have him racing off as fast as his little legs could carry him and a long one would see him return with all the speed he could command. He may not have been a true wolfhound but he certainly did his best.

"Hund is proving useful after all," I said to Morcant as we sat together one evening outside the workshop.

"Yes," said Morcant, "he may not look handsome but he makes up for it in other ways."

We little knew just how useful Hund was going to be.

Chapter Two
The Hayfield

"I knew it!" exclaimed the thane angrily as the messenger departed. "Didn't I say?"

"Indeed," murmured Morcant politely.

"You heard what he said! The Viking raids have started again. There is a new band of the pirates fresh from overseas camped on the banks of the Thames. Now all they need to do is join up with their old leader, Guthram, and the whole thing will erupt again."

"But this time we will be prepared," said Morcant, thinking of the king's new fortifications, "*if* Guthram does break his word and join with the raiders."

"Can't trust a fellow like that! Once a Viking always a Viking," said the thane. "I know what you are thinking, Master Morcant, but you are just too saintly. I've said it before and I'll say it again, Baptised or not, I do not trust Guthram – or Athelstan or whatever he calls himself these days. And just as we are about to start hay-making," he went on without listening to Morcant's mild protests, "and half the able bodied men are already away serving in the King's fyrd on their military duties. And talking of hay-making that reminds me – have you heard about the damage to the hay field by the river?"

Morcant shook his head. "Damage?" he said with raised eyebrows.

"It's strange," continued the thane. "Something has grazed the whole field completely and all along the river bank the ground is trampled into mud as though by some ... huge beast."

"Has anyone seen anything? When did it happen?" asked Morcant in surprise. "No one let cattle into the field – or horses?"

"No, no, I've made extensive enquiries but no one has been allowing their animals to graze there. Everything is out on the marsh with the cowherd as usual. Keep an eye out, can you, and let me know if you have any ideas?"

He turned to me now, more concerned about other things for the moment, "Wulfgar, we are going to need more ash wood spears. The king has asked for more weapons to go with our men when they change over with those already serving in the fyrd. I will make sure you have Swefred's services and you must turn out enough for all our men and to spare."

I thought to myself gloomily that Swefred would not be much help. His mind was definitely not on his job at the moment. Hund had gone missing. Swefred had searched for him all over the village but he was nowhere to be found. The boy's distress was pitiful. To him Hund was more than a dog, he was a friend that he had rescued and trained to such usefulness that the bond of loyalty between them was a two way thing. He spent every spare minute searching for the lost dog and the minutes that were not spare were clearly occupied mostly with thinking about Hund's disappearance – whatever Swefred's hands were doing.

The thane dismissed us and Morcant and I left the hall together.

"I'd better check my stocks of ash," I said.

"If you are going down to the plantation to look at the saplings," said Morcant thoughtfully, "you might take a look at that hayfield the thane mentioned – it sounds rather strange to me."

I was about to explain to Morcant that I had been thinking about checking over my stocks of seasoned wood, not growing saplings, when it occurred to me that I might wander down to the plantation by the river in any case. For one thing, I was curious about the hayfield. I did not admit, even to myself, that I was also keen to go because I was on the look out for Hund. It was not only Swefred who was fond of Hund; the dog had wormed his way into my heart and I was missing him.

"I'll do that," I said simply and set off towards the river.

I saw no trace of the missing dog on my way to the stand of young trees. The thane had been quite right about the hayfield, however. This particularly lush meadow sloped gently down to the river bank and was usually a productive spot. The grass had been long, ready for hay making, but there would be no crop now. It had been devoured. It was not nibbled short as if by sheep nor was it grazed as if by cows but it was almost torn up by the roots. I strolled down to take a closer look at the river bank. The wide river ran deep, still swollen by the torrential rains we had had earlier in the season. To my mystification there was a long swathe of grass here that was flattened rather than torn up. I walked round it slowly examining the area. At each end the flattened patch tapered off and towards one end the river bank itself was damaged, battered and torn into a slippery mass of mud and loose stones.

A thick tangle of trees and vegetation grew on the far bank where no one had tamed the land or broken it with the plough and I had often stood and gazed at its impenetrable vastness knowing that before we Saxons came and settled in Leofham, the bank where I now stood had been the same. My people had struggled to win, from this dark wilderness, food, shelter and home. It must have been a task that drained every particle of strength, ground down every grain of courage. But today, as I lifted my eyes from the flattened meadow grass to look across the broadly flowing river at the still unconquered forest, something unusual met my view. I strained my eyes. No, I was definitely correct. On the other side of the river, for a large distance, the lower trees and shrubs had been stripped of their leaves.

"What do you make of it?" I asked Morcant that evening as I joined him for supper. Eanflæde and the children had been listening to my account of the hayfield and were so mystified that there was an unusual quiet around the table except for the youngest, baby Modig Morcantson, who was banging his wooden spoon energetically to attract Eanflæde's attention to the fact that he wanted more pottage. Morcant did not answer at first, concentrating instead on the contents of his own bowl.

"Not animals from Leofham," he said at length, "not sheep, not cows ... If whatever it is is not seen by daylight I think it's time someone kept a watch one night to see what is going on."

"Everyone's busy," I said, thinking of the tired villagers coping with hay-making, shearing, and the second ploughing of the fallow ground. How could they be asked to stay up at night to keep watch on the field by the river and then carry on working at full strength again as soon as there was enough light to see by the following day?

"Well, looks as if it's going to be you and me then," said Morcant. "It's a full moon tonight and the sky is clear; what do you say?"

"You be careful," said Eanflæde suddenly. "I've heard tell of dragons and such like appearing when there's weather like that we've been having lately!"

I smiled, thinking of the old, old tale of Tiu and the dragon of Leofham. "I'll come," I said to Morcant, "although I wish we had Hund with us if we are going to encounter dragons!"

I returned to my workshop thinking to get a couple of hours sleep before Morcant and I set out on our adventure. I had left Swefred sawing up rough planks ready for repairs to a barn and was surprised when I walked through the door to see that quite a number of planks were still unsawn. "Swefred," I called, irritated, "where are you? Why haven't you finished your work? Don't you know we've a loom to repair for the lady Edith now as well as everything else? I need those barn planks done! "

"I'm here, Wulfgar, I'm sorry," came Swefred's voice from a corner, "O look, Wulfgar, poor little fellow – he's dying!"

I hurried over. Cradled in Swefred's arms was Hund – or what was left of him.

Chapter 3
Hund Again

Hund had never been a pretty sight, in fact, as a dog he was frankly hideous. Now, however, it was hard to even recognised that he *was*, or perhaps *had been*, a dog. All that was left was a limp bag of matted hair and blood and a pair of listless, clouded eyes. I prised aside the rags in which Swefred had wrapped him. A huge gash, dried and crusted over, ran down one side of the poor animal and one of his legs hung twisted and lose.

"Carry him to your mother, quickly," I said. "She may be able to save him."

I gathered some clean rags, settled the limp remains in them and handed the bundle over to Swefred. He set off carefully with his precious burden. I knew I would have little chance of sleep until I found out what on earth had happened to the dog. I finished off the remains of the sawing I had asked Swefred to do and then collected together such things as I thought I might need for our vigil after dark. Putting them handy by the door, I took myself off back to Eanflæde and Morcant's hut to find out how things were going with Hund.

You had to hand it to Eanflæde, she knew what she was doing when it came to injuries. I don't know what she had poured into Hund but by the time I arrived he was looking much less of a hopeless case.

"Will he live?" I asked.

"I'm not sure," she answered, her hands never pausing in

twisting her spindle and teasing out the fleece as she spoke, "but I think there is a chance he will. The injury to his side is long and nasty but it is not as deep as it looks. I have tied up his leg; I think the bone is broken. We will have to see how it goes."

Swefred was dribbling milk and water into Hund's mouth from his finger, closing the dog's mouth gently with his hand after each drop until he was sure it had been swallowed. It seemed slow work but after a while Hund's tongue appeared questing after the precious drops of liquid.

"Look, Wulfgar!" he whispered in delight, "he's getting better."

"Where did you find him?" I asked.

"I didn't," said Swefred. "He made his way home."

"In that state?" I exclaimed in surprise.

"Yes, it seems incredible but he had dragged himself right up to the door before I found him. I'm sorry I've not done all the work – I was nursing him, trying to get him to drink but I didn't know how to do it until Mother showed me."

I waved aside the thought of the timbers for the barn. "Have you any idea where he's been?" I asked. "He's covered with mud yet we've had no rain for a while and the ground is pretty dry everywhere."

"He's been by the river then, hasn't he?" came Morcant's voice from the fireside, "and I think it is high time we investigated what is going on there."

He was right, of course. I had seen plenty of fresh mud churned up along the bank of the river. It was the only place Hund could have gone to come home in such a state.

By the time Morcant and I set off the sun was setting and the moon was beginning to rise. Morcant's idea was to get ourselves into position to watch, ideally behind some sort of shelter, before the last of the sunlight vanished. There was still not a cloud in the sky and we chose our place with care. Just beyond my stand of young ash trees and not far from the river bank there was a dense clump of bushes and tough brambles.

"This'll do," whispered Morcant. "We will be well screened but there is an excellent view in all directions," and he led the way behind a corner of the clump, where we could hide and yet still see almost the whole field.

The full moon had now risen, a brilliant silver disc above our heads that lit up the whole scene as if it were daylight. The night was not cold and there was no hint of a breeze. I found I could sit down on the dry grass quite comfortably with my tunic belted round me. There was no sign of anything happening and the night was still and quiet. I watched a few bats skimming over the water on their evening hunt. My head began to nod ...

"Wulfgar!" came an urgent whisper that jolted me back to wakefulness, "Wulfgar, listen, what's that?"

I strained my ears. All seemed quiet, the bats were still skimming back and forth over the river questing for their supper. Then, over the water floated a sound of movement, of slight leafy rustling and the cracking of twigs, not directly nearby but somewhere deep among the trees. To the left of our hiding place there was a slight gap in the woods on the other bank and it struck me now for the first time that it might extend into the forest itself. I nudged Morcant and pointed to it and at that moment the sounds became clearer and more distinct – something was making its way through the forest to the river bank.

The bats vanished. The sound of something making a leisurely progress through the forest grew more audible. Morcant and I strained our eyes and I thought I caught sight of movement in the moonlit gap in the trees – could I see a snake? I whispered to Morcant, he shook his head and stared again at the spot. Suddenly he clutched my arm. A head, like that of some giant snake, was bent down, drinking from the river on the other bank.

Chapter Four
In The Moonlight

Tales of evil snake-like creatures that I had heard in the stories of the old gods came flooding back to my mind. I felt a strong impulse to take to my heels and flee while I could, but Morcant was gripping my arm with excitement. The snaky head was lifted from the water and as it rose we became aware of a vast bulk behind the sinuous neck. The whole creature became visible now in the bright moonlight as it stepped forward on thick, solid legs into the water. It paused for a moment and then turned with its head facing upstream and raised as though calmly contemplating the disk of the moon. I had never seen a living thing of such a size. It would have dwarfed any one of our village huts completely. The small head and long neck swelled out into a vast belly and then the rest of its body dwindled down into a long tail, the end of which carried a vicious club from which projected short, stout, wicked-looking spikes. There was no doubt about what we were looking at now.

As we gazed in fascinated horror, the dragon lowered its head and began to drink from the flowing river. Then, having had its fill of water, it moved slowly round and began tearing up mouthfuls of long grass and weeds on the bank. After that it turned its attention to the undergrowth on the opposite bank and, stretching with ease over the tops of the small trees and shrubs, it began stripping them of leaves. The river flowed round its massive legs, as if they were the buttressed pillars of some gigantic stone bridge, while it grazed placidly. Absurdly, I found myself wondering how long it would be before it discovered my precious stand of young ash trees and reduced them to stumps and bare branches.

I don't think we would have wanted to move even if we had dared to do so. The dragon was so terrible and yet so majestic and so completely at ease in the moonlight that we could not tear our eyes away from it. Never before or since have I seen a living creature of such proportions yet it moved with a tranquil grace that was mesmerising. I lost all count of time and the moon sank lower in the sky. The dragon continued to browse contentedly along the waterline. At last, as the moon shadows lengthened, it climbed unhurriedly out onto the bank of the river and began settling itself down on the ground, arranging its neck and tail around its huge bulk just as a dog might do. Its head was towards us now and we could see its eye, red and glowing in the gathering darkness.

Morcant and I still did not move a muscle. I wondered how fast a dragon could move – should we make a run for it? I raised an eyebrow towards the village but Morcant gave an almost imperceptible shake of the head. The dragon seemed so peaceful now and its eye was slowly closing; perhaps it would be best to wait until it was really asleep before sneaking off.

A light breeze sprang up and as we watched, a fox, on its way home from an evening forage, trotted out into the open meadow from the direction of the wind. Intent on making its way home, it seemed quite unaware of the dragon. The dragon, however, was well aware of the fox. The eye was suddenly bright and the tail twitched. The fox came on until the dragon's tail was almost under its nose. Then it evidently saw something move and, quite unconscious of the huge bulk attached to the tail, it crouched ready to spring. In a flash the tail lashed across, its horrible club ripping into the fox and flinging it high into the air. Lacerated and bleeding the fox landed almost at our feet beside the bushes that screened us. It had not had time to cry out; it lay dead on the grass. Now there was no doubt what could happen to us if we were discovered – and there was no doubt what had happened to Hund.

Morcant and I remained in the silence unable to move from our hiding place and (as far as I was concerned at any rate) unable to think what to do next. How long we waited I do not know but as the morning sky began to lighten, the dragon stood up slowly from its grassy nest. Then unhurried and stately, it stepped into the river and crossed to the far bank. We listened to the sound of it moving away down the gap in the trees, straining our ears until there was quiet again.

The silence was broken by the cry of a blackbird, "pink, pink, pink!" from somewhere in the woods across the river. Another blackbird answered and then in the bushes beside us a robin struck up his rich song. Morcant stood up and rubbed his stiff limbs. I followed, and in awed silence we made our way back to the village.

Chapter Five
Book Learning

Eanflæde, though horrified by what we had encountered, was not surprised. "Didn't I tell you?" she said to Morcant. "It may not be book learning but this is the weather for dragons!"

Morcant was looking through his library. This had begun with the copies of the gospels and other holy books found in the longship[6] but since times had become a little more settled it had started to grow. The king, as a mark of his special favour, sent volumes to Morcant from time to time as gifts. Morcant would always reply with loyal letters of encouragement and good advice to the king as well as a supply (when needed) of the precious frankincense[7] that eased the king's painful illness and warded off its debilitating attacks.

Now Morcant brought a smallish volume across to the table and turned the pages carefully, pages whose margins were entwined with images of familiar birds and animals in glowing colours. Here a donkey, there a pair of owls, a sheep, an ox...

"This is St Hilary's translation of Origen's gloss on *Job*," Morcant explained. "Beautiful, isn't it? But I have not found it useful before as we have an unglossed copy of *Job* here in the village. In any case Origen of Alexandria twists the holy patriarch's words into meanings which do not fit in at all with the teachings of the rest of the Holy Scriptures, I fear. Ah! This is the page I wanted, look!"

---

[6]See *Wulfgar and the Vikings*
[7]See *Wulfgar and the Vikings*

In the margins of the text the illustrator had drawn the very dragon we had seen! There was the bright-eyed head and long snake-like neck in the right hand margin. The sturdy legs and the huge belly took up the bottom of the page (humping up the words above it slightly as though the illustration had been drawn before the writing) and the tail rose up the left hand margin crowned with the evil-looking spiky club which had killed the fox at a single blow.

"He must have seen it!" I whispered, struck by the exactness of the illustration. "Where did this book come from, Morcant?"

Morcant shook his head, "I don't know, but who ever illustrated this copy of St Hilary certainly thought a dragon like this was the creature Job describes as Behemoth. The only concession the illustrator has made is to bend the tail upwards into the margin to fit his picture onto the page. The creature we saw did not raise its tail aloft – at least while we were watching last night. I wonder if the colours are accurate too? We were not able to see them properly in the moonlight." He bent his head, studying the picture carefully.

"Never mind about what colour it is or what it does with its tail!" exclaimed Eanflæde giving her spindle an impatient twirl as she worked. "What are we to do? The village is in grave danger if a dragon like that is wandering around nearby." An awful thought struck her as she wound the new spun yarn onto the spindle and she shuddered. "What if this creature has a brood of young ones born nearby?"

"Not born," murmured Morcant absently, still studying the picture, "hatched – dragons all lay eggs. Do they chew the cud I wonder?"

"But what are we to *do*?" said Eanflæde, no doubt thinking that the creature's digestive system was hardly to the point. "This thing is roaming about here – any of the children could suffer the same fate as Hund! What happens if it comes into the village? We should alert the thane at once."

"I think," said Morcant, "there is little we can do. The dragon is clearly only interested in plant food; it is a grazing animal like a cow. It only attacked the fox because it assumed (correctly, I think) that the fox was about to sink his teeth into its tail. No doubt Hund charged into the attack in his usual exuberant way – size would mean nothing to that dog – and received similar treatment. If we leave it alone and do not threaten it, I think it will not do any immediate harm."

I thought to myself that the thane was unlikely to see things in the same light. One hay field had already been lost. The village simply could not afford to lose more of its precious food supply. It was not possible to explain to the dragon that we in Leofham would be quite happy to welcome it so long as it confined its appetite to the opposite bank of the river!

I voiced my concerns and Morcant nodded, "You are right, of course, Wulfgar. But we do not know whether the dragon will change its habits again and start to devastate more of our land or whether it will be content to graze in the forest and just come to the river to drink and rest. It would be a shame to drive it away or injure it and perhaps lose men in the attempt, if it was in fact possible to live alongside the creature without danger."

His wife was aghast but I knew how Morcant was thinking. The scholar in him overruled more practical concerns for the moment and I could tell that, despite the danger, he longed to study the creature. Not only that, he hated needless killing, and this particular animal was the most impressive creature either of us had ever seen in our lives. "You did not see it, Eanflæde," I explained haltingly, "it was ... it was so regal, so dignified ..."

"*The chief of the ways of God*," said Morcant quietly, "that is how the writings of the patriarch Job describe such a dragon, my dear, and we, perhaps, should accept it as such."

"Will you convince the thane of your point of view?" I asked Morcant, thinking as I said it that Thane Pelhere would be unlikely to opt for a such a passive approach as he was suggesting.

"No," said Morcant, and there was the slightest curl to his lip as he spoke, "he would not understand – at least not yet. He is a man of action, not of learning – he still thinks of reading itself as something of a miracle. I think we should take it on ourselves to do a little more dragon watching before we mention what we have found to the thane. Eanflæde, you must be sure not to breathe a word of any of this yet."

"You mean you are not even going to tell him what we have seen?" It was my turn to be shocked now. "But, Morcant, it is our duty to report this! 'Take it on ourselves!' But the thane has asked us – ordered us – to keep a look out ... to report to him ..."

For a moment a very slightly guilty look crossed Morcant's face but it was gone in an instant and the composed face of the collected, wise scholar consulting his books and coming to his own conclusions, returned.

"Pelhere is a good man, but he is, well, hardly learned – what does he know of dragons? No harm will come of delaying for a little while, and I – we – may never get an opportunity of studying such a creature again," he said. "Wulfgar, will you come with me to watch again tonight?"

I felt torn. I could see Morcant's logic. But I also knew the thane must be told at once. I had been a fyrdman in battle and a fyrdman has to obey his thane. I knew just how serious disobedience to superiors was and what awful consequences could follow. The thane was our superior to whom we owed complete allegiance and who owed his own allegiance to the earldorman who in his turn owed allegiance to the king. To disobey Thane Pelhere was, in effect, to disobey the king himself.

"Morcant," I said, "you know as well as I do that the thane's orders are final. We cannot just take the law into our own hands. If we break our loyalty to Thane Pelhere then we are no better than Vikings ... not to be trusted!"

Morcant's round face settled into a determined expression that

I had never seen there before. "I am a scholar," he said and his voice was still quiet. "An opportunity to study a creature like this comes but seldom and not to many men. I will not give it up. Once this dragon is dead who will know if it could breathe fire? Who will know how it moves, what it eats? I am not suggesting we *never* tell the thane. All I want is long enough to make a proper study – then we can tell him everything he needs to know."

"If we do not obey *promptly*, we are *disobeying*," I said, still thinking of my time with the fyrdmen, "I remember at Edington, when the battle was at its height, the king ordered Earldorman Æthelnoth with our Somerset fyrd to move up towards ..."

"Yes, yes," interrupted Eanflæde impatiently, no doubt not wishing to hear another of my over-long war-time reminiscences, "I'm sure you are right, Wulfgar. Morcant, I can't believe what I'm hearing! Not even tell the thane? You may be a scholar but to disobey ..."

"Not a word!" said Morcant in a level and firm voice, "not yet. Will you come, Wulfgar? Or must I go alone?"

I struggled with my conscience. The thane ought to know. I pushed conscience into the background along with the story of the Battle of Edington. On a practical level I thought of the pile of jobs, the ash spears to ward off the approaching Vikings ... Swefred would just have to work harder. "I'll come," I said.

Eanflæde's yarn broke and the spindle dropped onto the earth floor with a dull thud. As she picked it up and teased out the fleece to rejoin the break she muttered, "I've heard that you cannot just go and *kill* a dragon, in any case. They're not ordinary creatures, dragons." It was as though suddenly she had changed sides.

Chapter 6
Swefred

When I arrived at the workshop Swefred was in a more cheerful mood. Hund was recovering now and, dragging his bandaged leg behind him, was trailing round the workshop after him.

"Swefred," I began, "you and I are going to have to work extra hard over the next few days. We need to make all the spears we can from the ash timber we have left as fast as we can. You are going to have to learn how to do it so that I can spend some time about some business Morcant and I have on hand – for the thane." ("Not quite true, is it, that?" said my conscience but I pushed it back down again,) "I'll show you exactly what to do and then you can set to work."

With Hund by his side Swefred worked with a will, learning what was needed quickly and without too much difficulty. I left him when I was satisfied he was producing good results and not wasting timber. I was too tired to carry on without sleep, especially if I was expected to do another stint of dragon watching at nightfall.

"I need somewhere to sleep for a few hours," I explained to Eanflæde. "I've left Swefred working his way through a pile of jobs with instructions to put the pot on for my supper but I'll have to shake down with Morcant unless I can tell Swefred what's going on."

"I still wish I knew what happened to Hund," said Swefred, as we shared our supper that evening. "I can't work out how he managed to get lost and injured."

"He is a brave dog," I said, trying not to get led onto the subjects I did not want to talk about. "Do you think he could have attacked something a bit too big for him?"

"Like a wild boar, you mean?"

"Perhaps," I was non-committal.

"I don't like to keep him tied up."

"I think you may have to, though, if you cannot be sure he will not go off seeking adventures again."

"Maybe he will learn his lesson. In any case he can't get far at the moment and Mother says he may always be lame now."

"Maybe."

"Wulfgar, why did God let him get so terribly injured? He will have a miserable life if he cannot get about properly any more."

I put down my bowl and looked thoughtfully into the fire.

"God does care for all his creatures," I said. "It is us, mankind, who have sinned and dragged the whole creation down with us. When creatures like Hund feel pain or even fight each other they are feeling the effects of our fallen state."

Swefred reached down and fondled Hund's ears. "Poor Hund," he said, "I do wish you had not wandered off and got lost."

"We are no different to Hund in that respect," I said. "In the holy books of God's Word we read that we have all gone straying away from God."

"You are straying a bit just now!" said my conscience. "What about your duty to tell Thane Pelhere what you saw?" but I pushed it back down firmly where it belonged in the background with the Battle of Edington.

"That's what my step-father, Master Morcant, says," said Swefred, and his tone was suddenly bitter, "but it sounds unfair to me, Wulfgar. Why should we be accountable to God for our lives? We never asked to be born."

"God is our maker and our Lord and Master, to whom we are responsible," I explained, ("Just as you and Morcant are responsible under God to the thane," said my conscience. I gave conscience another firm shove and tried to carry on) "yet we all try to live as if we were not accountable to him. The sinful nature which is within us from birth makes us rebellious. If we remain in that state we are lost. We have wandered off into danger just as Hund did." It sounded dead and lifeless and it was. Looking back now I'm not surprised that Swefred was not convinced. His face changed from bitter to angry.

"Well then, maybe God did make the world perfect and maybe we human folk did spoil it but I don't see why God doesn't do something about it. Why should animals - and people - go on suffering? If God is the all-powerful one he could put it all right again but he doesn't; it just goes on forever - death and suffering, suffering and death." He stood up, "My stepfather goes on and on about God's goodness – I don't see this *goodness* everywhere – and now you're at it too!"

I paused as I scraped the last morsel of pottage out of the bowl. Swefred's own father had died in a tree felling accident and somehow he had never quite accepted Morcant. I felt sorry for him. I wanted to say, "But God has done something for us. He sent Christ, the Redeemer, to bring us back to him!" but my conscience kept me grimly tongue-tied. Somehow it kept welling up from the background, where I tried to consign it, and interrupting me. I mumbled something or other about God's right to do what he pleased with his own creatures and Swefred scowled, scooping up Hund in his arms.

"Well, it doesn't make sense to me," he said and before I could answer he strode out with his dog into the gathering darkness.

Chapter 7
The Weather for Dragons

Morcant and I continued our secret dragon watching for several days. The pattern was always the same. The dragon appeared, enjoyed a drink of river water, browsed a little on bushes and trees at the water's margin and then rested in the meadow. No further damage was done to the Leofham crops and Eanflæde kept her mouth shut so no one else in the village, even her own family, had any idea of the fact that we had a new neighbour. I was uneasy. Not only was my conscience troubling me, I knew that sooner or later someone would find out – something so vast could not stay hidden forever – and once that happened Morcant and I could be in for big trouble for concealing the whole business.

My relationship with Swefred seemed to deteriorate. I wanted to talk to him about important things in life but whenever I tried it was the same. My conscience reminded me of what I was involved in. Swefred too seemed wary of anything but trivial conversation and even Hund's gradual recovery seemed to make no difference. All our former closeness had gone.

July arrived – the hungry month with old stores of food running out and new crops not yet in. Pottage got thinner and less satisfying and the endless, grinding round of crop weeding continued. Then out of the blue something happened that I had been dreading ever since the whole business of keeping quiet about what we had seen had begun.

"Some of the lads say they've seen a dragon!" Swefred burst into the workshop full of excitement, and more like his old self than I had seen him for weeks. "You don't believe that do you, Wulfgar?"

"Why not?" I asked cautiously, a feeling of foreboding welling up inside me.

"Dragons are out of the old legends," said Swefred. "They go with the old gods, Woden and Tiw and all the others, don't they? You and Morcant say they are made up creatures, don't you?"

I thought for a moment. "The Holy Books make mention of dragons so they definitely *were* real – even if they no longer exist," I began cautiously. "It is true that the old gods are not gods, but, you know, people must have got the idea of them from somewhere. They were probably just people – powerful kings or warriors in the old times. When people turn their backs on worshipping and serving the true God, they are driven to find something else to worship and quite often they choose their ancestors, those whom they have heard of from the past and whose great deeds are remembered. Perhaps if there really was a man called Tiw back long, long ago, he really did kill a dragon, if not here then somewhere else. It would be an event that would stay in people's minds long after it happened and even after they had forgotten the real Tiw and started to worship him as a god."

Then the cowherd reported the loss of a cow. She was one of the weaker animals and had a habit of lagging behind the rest of the herd. The cowherd had told the youngsters looking after the cattle to move them on to pasture further out in the marsh as the weather had been dry. Some of them had gone back when they found her missing and made a thorough search but could find nothing. Even then Morcant had not spoken, convinced there could be another explanation.

A few days later another animal was missed and this time the search did reveal something – and it was not a pretty sight. Tales were beginning to circulate in the village that a dragon was responsible.

"On the edge of the wood – just bloodstains and a few bones!" explained the thane, when we arrived, "completely devoured."

"Do you have any suspicions, my thane?" asked Morcant cautiously.

"I had been thinking of wolves," began the thane, "but that would be unusual at this time of year." He hesitated, "Have you heard any rumours, just among the lads and so on, of a ... dragon?"

Before Morcant could answer I said quickly, "One of the youngsters did mention that some of them were saying they had seen a dragon."

The thane nodded. "That's what I'd heard," he said.

"Do you have any kind of description, my thane?" asked Morcant.

"Yes," answered the thane, "but, you know, you can't trust what children tell you necessarily ... They say that, well, to summarise all the garbled things they were trying to say, it's almost as big as a hut, runs about on two legs, has a long tail, two smallish arms and a huge head with terrible teeth ..."

Morcant and I stared at each other.

"You seem surprised," said the thane. "Isn't that what you'd expect?"

"Are you certain the children are not making this up?" said Morcant, "to explain the disappearance of the cattle, I mean."

The thane considered. "I think it's unlikely," he said. "They may have been exaggerating but there are more plausible excuses they could dream up for their carelessness in losing cattle. I'd say if it was invention they would have been more likely to come up with wolves than a dragon."

There was a knock at the door and an anxious face appeared.

"What is it, henchman?" asked the thane.

"I've sent some armed men – the lads minding the cattle came running back into the village saying the dragon has come and is carrying off another cow into the woods."

The thane got up and reached for his sword and helmet. "I think it is time I went to see what is going on myself," he said. "Can you come with me, Morcant?"

"I'll come," replied the little Celt. "Wulfgar, could you go and explain to Eanflæde that I'm just helping the thane with a cattle problem?"

When Morcant returned to Eanflæde, I was still at their hut. He was very shaken.

"Whatever's the matter?" cried Eanflæde in alarm.

Morcant sat down by the fire. "It's hideous," he said. "It's a different sort of dragon completely, it's it's ..."

"Ah," said Eanflæde, looking wise, "they can change their shape you know, can dragons."

"Is everyone safe?" I asked. "It hasn't killed any of the thane's men?"

"No," said Morcant, "the thane's best woodsmen were called and we were able to keep down wind of it. We watched it devouring the cow without it being aware that we were there ..."

"Enough is enough," said Eanflæde firmly, "I don't care what you say. If cattle are disappearing – well, that's what dragons do! Only eats plants! Suppose it is one of the children next?"

The truth would have to come out now.

Chapter 8
The Dragon Hunters Set Out

The situation was far more complicated than even Morcant, for all his wisdom, had imagined.

"The longer you leave telling him about what you saw the other day, the worse it will be when you do have to own up," said Eanflæde, when Morcant was summoned to the thane's council the next day. "What good can it do to keep quiet about the fact that you've already seen the creature in another form?"

"Yes, you are right, my dear, it would serve no purpose now. Not to own up now would simply be cowardice," said Morcant. "You don't have to come with me, Wulfgar. It wasn't your idea to keep quiet."

"No, no," I'll come," I said. "I confess I'll feel a lot happier when I've admitted what we've been doing."

Morcant looked grateful, "If the thane has to hear all about it you'd be available to fill in anything I forget."

"What do you think will happen?" I asked as we made our way across to the thane's hall. "It's not really the same creature, is it?"

Morcant shook his head, "Creatures like dragons do not change their shape like caterpillars, whatever Eanflæde may tell you," he said, "but I imagine, after the sighting yesterday, the thane will want to organise a large force – muster everyone who can wield a weapon – and try to kill the creature."

"But could they do it? I mean, we've no idea ... this is not like the Vikings!"

"Indeed, *Lay your hand on him, remember the battle and do no more*, it says in the writings of the Patriarch Job," murmured Morcant. "This may not be a Leviathan but I think the same may apply."

"I'm organising a hunt immediately," began the thane. "The smith is making some of the strongest spearheads he can in readiness and a number of my best henchmen have already volunteered. Do you have, out of your wide experience, Master Morcant, any advice to offer – of a practical nature? I intend to ask you to call the village to prayer before we set out, of course."

"Where exactly do you intent to start your hunt?" asked Morcant.

"I was thinking we should start from the river bank, where there is evidence that the creature wrecked a hay field, and then work our way through the forest back towards where the creature emerged near where the cattle were grazing. I thought a pincer movement with men stationed there would allow the group that searched the forest, if they did not directly confront the creature themselves, to drive it towards the others in the open."

"My thane," answered Morcant, "I have been doing a spot of dragon watching of my own and I would ask you whether you consider it likely that a dragon that carries off cattle for food would also graze off grass, tree leaves and other vegetable food – as has clearly happened by the river bank?"

"Dragon watching of your own?" said the thane. "What do you mean, Morcant?"

"I have seen a dragon," began Morcant, "but I have to tell you that it is nothing like the creature we saw devouring cattle."

"Seen a dragon? When?" asked the thane sharply.

"For some weeks now I have been making a scholarly study of a dragon which emerges nightly from the woods, grazes on tree leaves on the opposite bank of the river, rests on our side and then returns to the woods on the other side at dawn."

Thane Pelhere was angrier than I had ever seen him in my life. "You've been seeing this thing regularly and not told me anything about it," he said in a level, quiet tone. "A dragon has been damaging our land, carrying off our cattle and endangering the whole village and you've been 'making a scholarly study' without telling me and after being expressly told to report on anything you see. Master Morcant, of Tyddewi, you have ill repaid the hospitality of Leofham ... and the high trust we have placed in you!"

Morcant looked down at his feet.

"You take too much on yourself, Morcant of Tyddewi, and it does not become you. Nor does it become the holy faith you profess. You are a Celt, subject of King Hyfaidd of Dyfed. You have sought and found protection from your enemies, the Vikings, at the hand of our gracious King Alfred. Here in Leofham..."

He broke off suddenly as though noticing me for the first time. "You are dismissed, Wulfgar, to go about your duties," he said sharply. "I will call for you later."

I opened my mouth to speak but he waved me away. This was not what I had intended. I had hoped to take at least my share of the blame and deflect some of the thane's wrath. Now I would have to make my own full confession to the thane at the first opportunity, assuming Morcant was not forced to explain my involvement, and I was not looking forward to it.

I did not have long to wait. I had been back at the workshop long enough to settle, rather moodily, into some work when Swefred appeared with a message that Thane Pelhere wanted to see me at once. I hurried back to the hall full of apprehension. Having served with the fyrdmen I knew that the penalties for disobedience were severe and swift and I half expected some of the thane's henchmen to have already taken Morcant away to confine him until he could be brought before the shire moot for judgment.

I was relieved therefore to find the thane sitting with Morcant, who although he seemed rather subdued, showed no signs of immediate punishment. I stood before the thane in the best military attitude I could muster, hoping he would take my loyal service with the fyrd into account when passing judgment.

"Morcant has told me the nature of your rôle in this business," said the thane, "and I am disappointed to find such behaviour among my serving fyrdmen ..."

Before he could go on, a henchman appeared, unaware of just what he was interrupting, "A messenger from the king, my thane, just arrived and asking to see you."

"Bid him enter and welcome – and, henchman, find him some refreshment."

The thane motioned Morcant and myself to stay and we shrank gratefully into a corner, glad of the interruption to the painful interview.

"What news? How fares the king?" asked the thane as the messenger entered.

"The king is well, I thank you, and sends his greeting to his loyal thane," he said. "I have messages and greeting from the king here," and he produced some sealed wax tablets. "I am to tell you that you will see from them that the king has been able to rob his heathen enemies of the element of surprise."

I knew that the Vikings liked to avoid giving battle to the king's army. Their tactic was to seize one of the king's Vills, surround it with earthworks and then ride out from it at will, plundering the neighbourhood and then running back inside as soon as the king's fyrdmen appear. This was why the king had transformed the fyrd from a temporary force, unable to besiege the Vikings through lack of proper supplies, into a mobile and regular force that did not have to be gathered together *after* the threat has appeared but would be ready for it.

The thane broke the seals and was casting his eye over the tablets. "Regular," he said, "that's what we are already doing, sending half our men out and then swapping them at the end of their tour of duty. Mobile. I see we now also have to provide horses for our fyrdmen when we send them. Supply. I see they now have to come also with provisions for sixty days."

The messenger nodded. "This is the price of keeping Wessex free," he said, "and the king makes no apology for it."

"I make no complaint to the king," said the thane, and then with emphasis and a glance at the two of us, "he has my *full and undivided loyalty*. Here in Leofham we are already keeping the peace and contending with dragons and whatnot without half of our fighting men ..."

"Dragons?" queried the messenger.

"Yes," said the thane, he paused, "I will read all this in detail as soon as I can. We will provide you with refreshment. Then you can tell the king that we will do our utmost to aid him in the battle to rid Wessex of the heathen Vikings and that we are doing our utmost to rid at least our part of Wessex of dragons also."

Thane Pelhere was reasonable as well as a capable leader of men. He knew that the slightest whiff of insubordination was serious enough to be treated severely and he found a way of making sure that every appearance of even handed discipline would be maintained. He managed it without depriving himself of a useful and loyal hearted cleric and also without condoning what had happened. The king's imminent visit gave him the opportunity. Reserving both of us to the king's judgment he trusted us both sufficiently to allow us our liberty until the king should arrive. We both expressed our gratitude, penitence and eagerness to help in the expedition to remove the dragon menace. Morcant gave every scrap of the evidence we had gleaned in our researches to the thane and he included Morcant in his council in the normal way when the plans for the expedition were made.

As a result, the party, when it set out that evening, did avoid the river bank area where Morcant and I had first seen a dragon. The thane was thoroughly puzzled by our description and seemed to think, like Eanflæde, that either the dragon could change its appearance or that we were somehow mistaken. However, Morcant persuaded him to ensure that his force of men was mounted as well as armed. As to tactics he could only suggest some sort of decoy animal and no one had any idea what kind of weapons would serve best against such a creature. It was a mixed and frankly nervous force that set out, Morcant and myself (as those who had studied the habits of at least some dragon or other) among them.

Chapter 9
Battle

Horses were not plentiful now in Leofham. I thought to myself, as I mounted the rather tired looking animal assigned to me, that if we were going to have to supply the king with mounted fyrdmen in future we might reach the point where we did not have enough to keep going.

Under normal circumstances I would have been eaten up with anxiety about what the king's judgment on our behaviour would be. I would have been racking my brains for suitable punishments and coming up with nothing, short of death or banishment, that seemed appropriate. But these were not normal circumstances. Instead, I found myself wondering what on earth we could do when confronted with a dragon. Although at the Battle of Eddington I had been nowhere near the front line, I had been training with the fyrdmen regularly and could handle a spear – at least I imagined I could – against the Vikings. But this seemed a thing so utterly unlike anything we had trained for as fyrdmen. I looked around me. The rest of the little force looked equally uncertain. The thane rode smartly to the front (he at least had a proper horse) and explained the plan of action.

"Now, the plan is to decoy the animal into the open," he explained. "This will give us the maximum opportunity. Before we set up the decoy I want you all settled well back into the trees and we will position the decoy so that the creature comes upon it first. You will be well down wind. The utmost silence will be preserved until I give the command. Everything depends on this and I know that, excellent woodsmen that you are, I can rely on you."

I thought of my sorry mount and wondered how much wood craft it had ever practised. Still, it seemed too tired to want to make any noise. I determined to do my best: that way perhaps I could show my loyalty and convince the thane that I had never really intended to disobey any orders. Then he would tell the king and perhaps I would get off lightly, perhaps we both would – if we survived ...

"You must all remember," went on the thane in a cheerful tone, "that this exercise is not unlike those we have successfully carried out in the past against wolves and that, although only one animal is involved here rather than a pack, the techniques needed will be similar."

Only one animal – I had my doubts even about that! The thane must have known that it was of a totally different order of threat to a wolf pack. I could see, however, the calming effect of his words on his men.

"Everyone is to prepare his mind, nonetheless," the thane continued. "No one will show a want of courage or mar the honour of Leofham. The sight of this creature may, although presenting a danger no worse than that of a wolf pack, seem more daunting because of its unfamiliarity and somewhat unusual size. I am completely confident that fyrdmen such as yourselves, many of whom are distinguished veterans of the great Battle of Eddington, will acquit themselves with their usual valour."

He made it sound simple and I noticed that the men around me seemed to grow more confident as they listened but then, unlike me, most of them had never seen a dragon.

"Above all," concluded the thane, "I know that you will all obey my orders efficiently and that no one, in the heat of the moment, will be tempted to disregard my commands whether or not they seem to run counter to your own ideas." I winced. "Above all you *must not* begin the attack on the creature until I give the signal. Is that clear? Master Morcant has studied the creature we are about to engage, both in books of learning and in the flesh, and I am confident that the plan we have worked out together will be completely satisfactory."

I raised my eyebrows ever so slightly and looked at Morcant. I knew neither he nor the thane had any real idea of how to tackle a dragon or even how to answer the questions which (as concern over my longer term future began to fade again before the present dangers) were rising in my mind. How fast could this dragon move and for how long? What weapon, if any, could pierce its skin? What vital part of its body should we aim for? Morcant gave no answering glance and I wondered what the others were thinking. It occurred to me that the more simple among them might wonder, as Eanflæde had done, whether a dragon could really be killed at all.

A rather elderly and skinny looking cow was led out as an unwitting sacrifice to the dragon and she seemed definitely to feel that whatever was going on was something in which she did not wish to participate. I looked round me again. The men were certainly looking more courageous now that they understood – or thought they did – what was expected of them. The thane gave the order and we moved off with impressive quiet to the fringe of woodland that had been selected. The cow, however, was anything but quiet and the whole forest must have known her whereabouts by the time she had been tied upwind of us. After a while, though, finding herself left alone tied up in a grassy place, she stopped bellowing and tugging at the rope and began to crop the grass. I patted the neck of my old horse reassuringly and as I did so I noticed something out of the corner of my eye; something, or rather someone, who should not have been there at all. Crouching at the back of the party, the faithful Hund like a shadow beside him, was Swefred.

I was furious. Yet another breach of discipline! Nothing could be done about it now, of course, here they were and here they would have to stay. But how could he! Without even asking me or Morcant, never mind Thane Pelhere! The thane would be bound to consider that he was following our bad example. Now there would be more trouble ahead than ever.

Waiting, especially for something frightening, is always difficult. We had not been settled among the trees for long, watching the poor old cow industriously grazing away, before my anger with Swefred began to subside and I started to feel that even the appearance of the dragon would be preferable to the stillness and silence. Would it come at all? How long would the thane make us wait before giving up? The sun was low in the sky and the trees cast a long shadow over the grass plot beside the river. As I sat I kept track of the passage of time by watching the shadow of an exceptionally tall tree as it moved towards a rocky depression in the centre of the grass. Nearer and nearer it crept as the sun sank. Perhaps when the shadow touched the edge of the little dip the thane would give the signal for us to go home. Then, with luck, Swefred and his dog could slink off unobserved. Perhaps ...

The cow stopped grazing and lifted her head. She took a few more mouthfuls and then looked up again uneasily. Then my old horse also pricked up its ears and took a slight step sideways.

I strained my eyes to look at the opposite side of the river and then I saw what they had sensed. The creature that was running towards us was nothing like the animal that Morcant and I had seen. It was over the river now, hideous on its two legs. With its great head uplifted it ran towards our decoy. Would the thane never give the signal? I could even smell it now, an evil stench like something decaying and rotten. The thing would be on us in a moment! The poor old cow stood no chance. The dragon picked it up, ripping the stake and cord out of the ground as it did so ... Pelhere's arm went up and in a split second the tension was broken – I found myself charging towards the monster.

A volley of spears – mine included – and then we were confronting the creature. Pelhere was shouting at us to dismount and had leapt from his own horse. "We have no chance!" I thought desperately as, enraged and indeed actually wounded (by some miracle at least one or two of the spears had done a little damage), it lunged at him. To my horror I saw that far from observing from the background, Swefred was close beside me.

"You stupid child!" I heard myself cry. "What on earth are you doing here, get out of this! Now!"

My horse joined the stampede of Leofham horseflesh that was rushing away from the scene with Hund alongside them. The dog was evidently showing his true colours, I thought, and they were those of a coward! Trying to forget about Swefred and Hund, I began to work my way round to get near the rear of the beast. Pelhere and three of his henchmen were engaging the dragon now at closer range, trying to parry its lunges with shields and making sword thrusts to its body. I changed my tactic and ran alongside to try to help and as I did so someone on my left gave a wild shout. At the same moment all the horses veered round and started galloping in a mad panic back towards us again.

At first I thought that it was not we but the dragons who had performed a pincer movement; the beast that Morcant and I had originally observed was coming briskly towards us over the grass. Then I realised that urging it on with yapping barks as though driving an erring sheep or cow was Hund! Neatly dodging the thrashing tail, now that he had first hand experience of what it could do, and with hardly a trace of a limp, Hund goaded the vast creature towards the scene of our struggle. Its appearance changed everything.

The dragon dropped the limp remains of the cow and with a low roar deep in its throat it turned to face the new arrival. It evidently regarded the newcomer as an interloper in its territory, compared with which we of Thane Pelhere's party were flies which could be brushed off later.

"Fall back!" shouted the thane moving towards our original position. "Draw off! Regroup!"

We did not need to be told twice. I for one did not want to be anywhere near that deadly tail.

The two legged dragon made a lunge toward its new enemy but it was too late. The tail had whipped across, lacerating and tearing into its legs so that it stumbled and tottered, then a second blow left it lying senseless on the ground. Hund had wisely withdrawn by this time and the second dragon, finding itself free from its annoying little tormentor as well as triumphant over its foe, turned and began to amble slowly back down the meadow and towards the river.

"Approach with extreme caution! It may only be stunned," commanded Pelhere as the vast bulk of the victorious dragon crossed the river and began to retreat unhurriedly into the forest.

He was wise to urge care and quite correct in his surmise. The huge jaws were still mobile and, as we approached, the creature began to try to struggle back onto its feet. As it did so, to my horror, I saw Swefred rushing at its head with what I thought must be a poker from the smithy. "Get back!" I yelled, Get back!" but it was too late. There was a horrible crack and Swefred was lying on the ground.

It was not without difficulty and some real moments of danger that Henchman Wilfred and a couple of his men succeeded in hacking off that hideous head. The prone form of Swefred lay in their path adding to their difficulties.

The thane sent some men to round up the horses, "Someone get a hurdle or something to carry this child back home on," he commanded, then looking after the monster that was vanishing into the trees across the river. "So there *were* two of them! Where is that courageous dog?"

Hund was crouching by Swefred, anxiously licking his master's face and whining quietly. When a couple of henchmen arrived with a length of fencing from nearby and started to ease Swefred onto it, he growled and snarled at them until Morcant caught hold of him and whispered something soothing into his ugly ear.

"Should we go after the other dragon, Thane Pelehere, Sir?" queried the one of the henchmen. "Hardly seems right after what's happened!"

Chapter 10
Dragon-slayers

One of the things I admired most about Eanflæde was her courage in a crisis. Many another mother would have thrown her apron over her head and given herself up to grief on seeing her son brought home in such state but Eanflæde was the same competent, dependable person with Swefred as she was with any other sick or wounded villager. Swiftly, with her mouth set in a grim line, she tore up bandages and organised hot water. Firmly she ordered the younger children to go to her neighbour across the way and, sending her eldest daughter to the chest where she kept her herbs and ointments, she cleaned the wounds – deep punctures in the shoulder, back and leg from those horrible teeth – anointed them and bound them up. She worked silently while Morcant and I stood foolishly by and she never once reproached us for letting Swefred get involved or blamed us for not heeding her warnings about dragons. Hund obviously trusted her completely – with good reason from his own experience – and to my amazement he moved away from Swefred, lying down by the fire with a soft doggy sigh.

The thane sent for me the next morning – or rather he sent for poor exhausted Morcant who wanted me with him.

"What news?" he asked as we were shown in, "How's your stepson?"

"Eanflæde says he'll pull through, and I think she's correct, Thane," said Morcant quietly, "but it is too early to say how the injury will affect him."

"Eanflæde knows what she's doing," said Thane Pelhere, strategically ignoring the rest of Morcant's reply. "if she says he'll pull through, he will pull through."

Morcant nodded, grateful that the thane had been tactful enough not to say anything about the fact that Swefred should never have been with us in the first place.

"And I take back my harsh words about that dog!" said the thane. "However did he know what to do?"

"I'm not sure he did," said Morcant shaking his head and with the ghost of his usual smile. "Knowing Hund, I'd say he was just out for adventure with a touch of revenge!"

"Wulfgar," continued the thane, "we have decided to pursue the remaining dragon and Hund is obviously the dog for the job." He turned to the wax tablet open on the table before him. "The royal visitation is expected at New Year. We will be hard put to it now that the harvest is underway but I am hoping that we will be able to report to the king that we have rid the area of dragons – harvest or no harvest."

There was not a murmur from Morcant, although I knew this was contrary to his own ideas of what should happen.

"I'm not sure how Hund will behave without Swefred, Thane," I said.

"We need all the help we can get for this job," said the thane, "human or canine. Hund will have to do his best like everyone else!"

We crept quietly back into the hut and Morcant softly but firmly ordered Eanflæde to bed. "Wulfgar and I will take over now," he whispered and Eanflæde got up silently from where she was sitting, not even spinning, beside her son. I saw her lower lip tremble as she stumbled into their little curtained off sleeping space. Morcant, meeting her eye as she paused before disappearing, shook his head slightly as though to encourage her not to disobey his kindly and necessary order. His gesture was not needed. More wise than either he or I had been, Eanflæde knew, without his reminder, the necessity of loyalty to her own link in the chain of obedience that bound our society together.

Stretched out on a pallet, his arm and shoulder stiffly bandaged, Swefred was a pitiful sight. As Eanflæde disappeared, Hund got up from the fireplace. He stretched his stumpy legs carefully one by one and then moved over to sit beside Swefred. He evidently did not trust Morcant and me as much as he trusted Eanflæde. He sat beside his master for a few seconds and then gently licked the hand that hung limply over the edge of the pallet. Swefred's eyes flickered open for a moment and then closed again.

Morcant put a gentle hand on his forehead. "No fever, God be thanked," he whispered. "If we can keep him clear of that, he will indeed pull through. Can you sit here while I consult some of my books, Wulfgar?"

As I sat beside Swefred I considered how I had failed to tell him all the things I had wanted to say that evening just after Morcant had made his decision to carry on dragon watching without consulting the thane. Suppose he did not survive these injuries? I had not answered him properly because I was conscious of my own guilty involvement with Morcant's plans. At the time I had had no idea that perhaps it was my last chance to speak to him about such important things. Then it had made me feel uncomfortable but I had consoled myself with the thought that there would be other times. Now perhaps it was going to be too late! Was Swefred very soon to meet a Judge with more authority than Thane Pelhere or even King Alfred himself, and meet that Judge unprepared? If so, was I responsible for not speaking to him as I should have done? Another weight of guilt seemed to settle heavily on my shoulders.

But between them Morcant and Eanflæde kept fever at bay. Slowly but perceptibly Swefred clawed his way back from the brink. Before Morcant sent me home that evening, although he had not spoken a word, Swefred had reached out his hand towards his beloved Hund and Hund, his joy knowing no bounds, had wagged his stump of a tail until I thought it would fall off.

I struggled on with my work from day to day on my own; the barn planks, the loom, a cart with broken shafts. Whether Swefred would ever be fit to help me again was an open question but perhaps at least I would be able to put things right if only he survived. He made progress slowly, but even when he was able to sit up a little, Eanflæd would not let him talk more than absolutely necessary, shooing me away when I put my head round the hut doorway.

The issue of what to do with the carcass of the dead dragon was pressing. The stinking remains could not really be allowed to stay where they were for ever but the thane was naturally keen that some memento of the great exploit should be preserved – and not just until the king's visit. It was obvious that he was going to enjoy telling King Alfred all about the battle and also that he wanted some durable evidence of the creature's size and ferocity. Morcant, as the only person in the village with any artistic pretensions, was ordered to produce some drawings before the carcass deteriorated too much to be of any use as an *aide-memoire*. After the king's visit some attempt might be made to remove the corpse to a suitably distant spot. The thane also insisted that some of the largest bones should be preserved permanently but he was reluctant to separate them from the carcass until that king had seen the whole extent of the creature for himself.

I walked down to the scene of the battle with Morcant who wanted to do some sketches on the spot. As we approached the river however it became obvious that he would have to be quick. A cloud of carrion birds arose as we approached.

"They'll have it picked clean in no time," said Morcant, settling down on a rock with a piece of charred stick and some boards borrowed from my workshop, "and a good thing too!"

Holding my nose, I stepped round the huge beast to where the head still lay where it fell.

"We ought to do something with that head," said Morcant from his perch on the rock. "Whoever heard of a dragon-slayer not carrying off the head?"

"I don't know what you would do with it," I replied thoughtfully, "and the thane wants as much as possible left here intact to impress the king."

I studied the head closely and an idea formed in my mind. In my workshop was a big baulk of timber, unsawn and unused, that was a rather unusual shape. Something had distorted the tree in its growth and this twisted piece of timber should have been discarded for firewood but I had taken a fancy to it. I studied the head of the dragon closely. In my mind's eye that piece of timber was taking a certain shape ... but I was so busy working on my own ... it would be hard to find the time ...

We were blessed with exceptionally fine weather that August and the wheat and rye and then barley and oats were all brought in without damage. But despite thorough hunts of the woodland across the river, in which Hund participated, reluctantly at first, no trace of the remaining dragon could be found. As September and the New Year approached the thane became more frustrated. Villagers who would rather have joined their families gleaning in the cleared fields or making an early start on threshing were sent off in parties to look for the creature. At length, however, the thane called off the hunt, allowing the men to get on with harvesting the peas, beans and vetches before the king arrived.

A tousled head appeared round the door of my hut one morning as I was working away on yet another urgent cart repair. "Swefred's asking for you! He's loads better." It was one of Eanflæde's brood, excited and pleased. I put down my tools: the cart would have to wait.

Swefred was indeed looking better and sitting on a bench with his back against the wall. His arm, free of bandages, was in a light sling. He stood as I entered and took a few steps towards me.

"Swefred!" I cried, delighted to see him so much better, "you really are on the mend."

"Yes and I need to apologise to you," he began at once.

"To me?" I replied rather surprised. "I think it's Morcant and your mother who deserve the apology not me!"

"I have spoken to them but I need to tell you too," he said. "I should never have taken that poker and sneaked off after the dragon hunters."

"That's true," I replied, wanting to be honest about his actions, however guilty I felt about mine, "but I think the casualty rate might have been higher and the dragon still living if you had not been there."

He looked surprised.

"Without Hund," I explained, "we would have been in trouble."

"Oh, but Hund would have been there anyway," said Swefred. "I was only there because I went after him to fetch him back. He'd run off to join in and by the time I found him it was too late to go home again."

I was about to express my own apology for having thought Swefred's presence at the hunt to have had quite different motives but he went on quickly. "There is something else I've spoken to Morcant about too. Do you remember that time ... before the dragon hunt, I mean, when you spoke to me about ..."

I could indeed remember. While Swefred had been so ill, I had thought of little else.

"I did you a disservice that day," I said. "I should have told you so many things but I let the opportunity slip."

"I think I knew those things already," said Swefred, "but I was unwilling to accept them. I didn't want to listen to Morcant and I didn't want to hear the same things from you either. I think I knew what you were going to tell me but I was feeling angry. You know how my father died – he was so dear to me. He had me working alongside him even though I was still young. He had time for me and always listened to me and talked to me. Losing him was bad enough but I was learning to swallow my grief and live with it. Then mother married Morcant and I hated it – not Morcant himself really, he's always been decent to us all – but the situation. I didn't want someone trying to take my father's place. Then there was the baby, that was worse still somehow. But just when it all seemed black and horrible there was Hund. He loved me and needed me. I'm not making excuses, Wulfgar, but that made it so awful when he disappeared and got hurt."

I nodded, suddenly hopeful that despite my botched attempt to tell him what he needed to know, Swefred had come to see his situation as it really was – and dealt with it as I had hoped he would.

"I was angry with God," he continued. "I know it sounds awful – but I could not understand why everything always went wrong when God could put it right."

"And then things got even worse," I said. "You were injured yourself."

"No!" said Swefred, "that's the strangest thing of all, Wulfgar. You'd have thought I'd have been more angry than ever – especially with God. And I was at first. But then something came into my mind that I'd heard Morcant reading from the Holy Book of Jeremy the Prophet. Do you remember? God told him to go and watch the potter – Morcant said it was exactly the same as Frithestan across the road from here who makes all our jugs and bowls. Then I thought about that table we made, Wulfgar, do you remember it? You and I, we decided the legs needed to be shorter because it was for old mother Ætte and she's not very tall to say the least! We cut a good few inches off all the legs and the table itself had no say in the matter! In fact the idea was so comical that, ill as I was, I actually laughed – just quietly – I think my poor mother was worried that I'd lost my reason as well as everything else! And no sooner had I realised that – before I had time to wonder how I was going to shoulder the burden and carry on taking the blows heaven was dishing out or anything like that, other things popped into my mind one after another like a sort of procession – idea after idea, truth after truth that I should have understood and yet hadn't because I'd shut my mind to it all. Am I making sense, Wulfgar?"

"Perfect sense," I said, hardly daring to interrupt him with a reply.

"You see, I was too ill to keep my mind shut any more and the ideas – the things I knew really in my heart of hearts – came crowding in until I wanted to cry out loud but my voice wouldn't work well enough – yet. Of course, I had understood what you'd been trying to tell me that day when I didn't want to listen. I just didn't like it. Now I realised that God does shape all things, even me. The shaping was painful but I suddenly wanted it to be for my good. I wanted it to be God dealing with me so that I did not turn my back on him any more. I wanted to belong to him just as you do and my stepfather does, to be forgiven, to be one of his children."

I nodded, still not wanting to speak.

"I think you can guess the rest, Wulfgar."

"I think I can."

Chapter 11
Dragon Bones

Just before Michaelmas a messenger arrived to say that the king was not far behind him and that he would be bringing good news of victory over the Vikings with him. The thane began making preparations and Morcant and I were called to the hall – rather to my surprise as I knew we were in disgrace.

"I have decided on a suitable gift for the king," explained Thane Pelhere to me. "I would like you to turn a drinking cup for the king and decorate it with carved dragons to celebrate the recent defeat of the monster by the men of Leofham."

Morcant nodded, more confident of my abilities than I was, and the thane began to discuss other preparations for the king's visit. He was still torn between removing the largest of the dragon's bones that formed the huge back legs and setting them up in the hall and leaving the monster intact for the king to inspect. Together we walked down to the dragon's remains. It had taken little time for the carrion birds to remove almost every last vestige of flesh, leaving the bones to bleach in the late summer sun. It was certainly an impressive sight. The creature's remains lay spread out on the ground, the larger bones unchanged in position from the day it died.

"It might be possible," mused Morcant as he looked at it, "to remove those two huge leg bones that are uppermost without disturbing the skeleton as a whole too much."

"Indeed," said the thane eagerly, glad to think that his hall could be decorated with this vast trophy when the king arrived and yet the creature's complete bulk would also be available for the king to inspect. "Henchman Wilfred can get some men over here to do the job today while the weather is fine."

"If, my thane, you were to have them set up so," said Morcant, shaping an inverted V with his arms, "you might have a good arch – against a wall on the dais – over your chair, for instance."

As for the cup, I knew I may not have long to complete the commission and I hurried off later in the day to see Morcant for advice and to look at his drawings of the dragon. That other piece of work I had started on would have to wait – again.

"I wish I could carve a picture of the dragon we did *not* kill on the cup," I said to Morcant later. "It would be a much easier shape and I can visualise it winding round a cup much better than the monster we *did* get rid of!"

"I don't think the thane would want to give the king a memento just of the fact that there is still a dragon lurking in the woods somewhere," said Morcant, "but I don't think we should be taking the credit for killing the other dragon either. Granted it met its final end at the hand of the men of Leofham, but without the dragon that got away we would never have managed to defeat it."

I nodded, "Perhaps I should put both dragons on the cup in some way," I mused, "that would be a better reflection of the true facts."

Among the villagers there was great anticipation of the royal visit and not only because the king was coming. Our fyrdmen would be coming home with him. Families were making their own welcome preparations which were as heartfelt as the thane's even if on a smaller scale. A fresh contingent of the Leofham fyrd would set out with the king when he left and I wondered if I would be one of them or whether another fate awaited me after the king's judgment.

The first time I had served as a fyrdman I had been all eagerness to set off. I had had no idea of what was awaiting me on the king's service and had a rosy picture of what life as a fighting man would entail. Now it was different. I was only too aware of the hardships, privations and dangers. I confess I would have been much less keen to go if even less pleasant alternatives were not staring me in the face. What would the king's judgment be? I worked away at the cup diligently, mulling over in my head my worries about what would happen to me. Gradually the vessel took shape and I did my best to make the dragons that adorned it both lifelike and impressive.

"Very true to life!" said Morcant when I showed him the finished cup, "and the two animals look suitably fierce. You know, you really are good at this sort of thing. Beside your work, my drawings of the carcass are hopeless. If the thane wants any more sketches I am going to ask him to go to you not me. The only thing you can't really show is the size. A bit difficult on a cup!"

"Perhaps I'd better get Hund on there too somewhere," I suggested, feeling flattered by the compliments. "That would at least give some comparison. I have left a band round the brim, look, for some letters, I thought there should be some inscription."

Morcant thought that an excellent idea.

"What do you think I should put?" I asked.

He thought for a moment. Then he went to the book case and reached down the precious copy of the book of the Patriarch Job. "This is just the thing," he said, after turning the pages, "ecce behemoth ... behold Behemoth whom I made with thee ..."

"Yes," I said, "that will do nicely." I took the cup from him ready to return to the workshop and carry out the improvement. At the doorway I paused.

"What do you think the king's judgment will be, Morcant?" I asked. "It is serious, isn't it – what we did I mean?"

He looked up from his copying desk. "Very," he said. "Let us pray that the king will be merciful."

"King Alfred is a merciful man," I said, "but he cannot afford to let insubordination go unpunished. He can't just pack me off with the fyrdmen, for instance, not knowing if I'll obey him in the heat of the battle."

"Indeed," said Morcant, and then he paused for a moment, his face serious. "What I did was wrong, Wulfgar, and I'm sorry for it now. I led you into ... into the sin of disobedience and I owe you an apology. I intend to make it absolutely clear to the king that it was on my responsibility that you were involved. I've asked God's forgiveness and I am at peace with him for myself. I am ready to take whatever punishment the king thinks fit to mete out." He paused again and I opened my mouth to try to tell him I understood and that I knew all along that I should have behaved differently. But before I could get the words out his face brightened and he said, "But I have reason to hope things will yet turn out better than you might think – for both of us."

More than that he would not say but I felt more at ease as I returned to the workshop.

Chapter 12
The King

When I had managed to squeeze Hund's portrait onto the cup, I took it back to Morcant for approval.

"It's just like him!" he said. "You really have a gift for this, Wulfgar! Can I take it with me to the thane's hall this morning? – in fact it would be better if you came too. The thane has the great bones cleaned and all ready to be set up and you would be just the person to oversee the job."

The thane was pleased with the cup but as for the bones, a great deal more than just overseeing was needed. I had to make some supports and fixings as well as advise on the position of the bones. It took a few days to get the job done but the king had still not appeared. Thane Pelhere was immensely pleased with the finished results. He stood in the centre of the great hall taking in the arch of huge bones that now surmounted his chair on the dais.

"Excellent, Wulfgar, excellent!" he exclaimed delighted. "This is as good as the cup you made and I'm sure the king will ..."

At that moment he was interrupted by a loud hammering on the hall door and when Henchman Wilfred opened it a breathless messenger tumbled in.

"Where ... is ... the ... king?" he demanded, "I have news ..."

"The king is not here yet," replied the henchman, "but we expect him at any moment. What are your tidings? Good or ill?"

"Good ... Sir ... good ..." panted the messenger at once, "but I must see the king, the Lady Ealhswith ..."

The thane advanced rapidly from the end of the hall. Henchman Wilfred ushered the messenger forward and he saluted the thane politely. "Ah! You have good news concerning the Lady Ealhswith, the king's wife," said the thane, his face wreathed in knowing smiles, "you are most welcome. The king is promised here shortly – perhaps today – so you need go no further in your search. Wilfred, please find the king's servant some refreshment."

It was not long before sunset that the royal party appeared, the king on a stately palfrey surrounded by earldormen and thanes carrying the royal standard and with our own dear fyrdmen marching behind him. They received a rapturous welcome and it was some minutes before the excited cheering and shouting subsided enough for the king to address his loyal Leofham subjects.

"My beloved people," he began, when the tumult had died down, "my beloved people, Let us give glory to Almighty God who has enabled us through his might to keep at bay the enemy."

There was a rustle among the crowd as heads bowed and children were quickly silenced.

"Where is Master Morcant?" said the king quietly and, as Morcant stepped forward to lead the assembled village – and his king – in prayer, the king too dismounted and bowed his head.

As soon as Morcant had finished speaking, the messenger stepped forward into the king's sight.

"What news, Entgar?" cried the king at once. "How is it with the Lady Ealhswith?"

The messenger leaned forward and spoke to the king quietly.

"God be praised!" exclaimed the king. "Thane Pelhere, we truly have reason to feast! My wife has borne me another son!"

How the messenger had kept this delightful news from the Lady Edith I could not imagine but she was as surprised and delighted as the rest of us as soon as she heard what the king had said. She kept quizzing the poor messenger about the baby's colouring, size, family resemblances and possible name, although he seemed to know little of such details.

My enjoyment of the ensuing feast was somewhat spoilt. Had Thane Pelhere told the king about Morcant and me? When would we be called for judgment? However, the occasion was indeed a joyful one for Thane Pelhere. The king was most satisfactorily impressed by the huge bones that formed the arch under which his seat had been placed.

"What creature on earth was that?" he asked the thane in astonishment. "Surely, you were not in earnest with your message about dragons!"

"Sire," replied Thane Pelhere, "those are indeed the rear leg bones of a dragon. It had been attacking our cattle but, as you can see, through the goodness of God and the valour of the men of Leofham, it is no more."

One of the thane's henchmen leaned over, "and not just the valour of the *men* either, Sire," he said. "You gave us a noble wolfhound bitch in pup and one of those puppies had the courage to tackle a dragon!"

Of course, the king insisted on hearing the full tale and the thane was only too glad to tell him although he seemed a little embarrassed when it came to Hund's part in the story – after all the king could have no idea what sort of puppy Hund had turned out to be.

"So I will have dragon-slayers among my fyrdmen when I depart from Leofham!" said the king, delighted by the whole adventure, "and you say one dragon is still at large? You know, when the Viking raiders commenced their attacks in Northumberland – when the first Aethelred was king of that realm – the chroniclers mention that dragons were seen before the attack. One of my Earldormen had a grandmother who actually saw them although he had no clear idea of what they were like – she died before he was born. Perhaps the Leofham dragons are a sign that the Viking menace is now coming to an end! Just as the first dragons were a portent that their dragon-prowed ships were arriving so this is a portent that they are departing forever. We must have a dragon hunt tomorrow, Pelhere! Where is this wonderful dog? I must meet him!"

There was an awkward silence.

"Come," cried the king, "surely he did not perish in the fray?"

"No, no, Sire," said the thane, "it is just that ... well, Sire, he is not the sort of dog you might expect, Sire."

"He would seem to be a credit to the wolfhound breed," said the king frowning. "Send for him, Pelhere."

Swefred was now well enough to get around, although his arm was still stiff and awkward. He was in a corner of the hall with Eanflæde and the younger children and when the thane beckoned to him he came up to the dais trembling with astonishment.

"Fetch Hund here at once," commanded the thane. "The king's wish is to see him."

Swefred vanished on his unexpected errand and soon returned with Hund trotting obediently at his heels. At a soft word of command from Swefred, Hund walked in front of him and stopped. Swefred spoke again and Hund stretched out his diminutive front legs, lowering his head while his master also knelt in front of the king.

The king took one look at the dog and burst into laughter.

"What have we here?" he exclaimed. "Well trained, yes, but this is no wolfhound – and yet ..." he studied Hund more closely, "... and yet I *think* I detect something about the coat and the eyes ..."

"All we can claim, Sire," murmured the thane, "is that his mother was a wolfhound. As to the rest ..."

Swefred and Hund were still kneeling before the king.

"Sire," the thane said, "the lad who has trained him will tell you, if you care to hear more of the dog's exploits."

"Rise, Dog-boy," said the king, "you have clearly trained some unpromising material well. From what I have heard the animal is a credit to his wolfhound breed – whatever his appearance."

Sire," said Swefred, in a firm but quiet voice, "by your leave, he is not a wolfhound, he is a dragonhound."

The king slapped his thigh, "Excellent!" he exclaimed, "Excellent! Pelhere, your village has its own breed of dog as well as its own dragon. Leofham is always full of surprises!"

It was indeed true, Morcant told me afterwards, that the Year of Our Lord 793, when the Vikings sacked the monastery of Lindisfarne in Northumberland, had been marked by the appearance of dragons. "Flying dragons, if my memory of the Chronicles is correct," he said, "but I do not think we have seen the last of invaders here in Wessex just because two dragons have appeared."

"I don't think the king thinks so really either," I said, "or he would not be making such detailed and costly preparations for defence."

The king and his retinue had been in conference with the thane all morning explaining more of his plans to unite and strengthen a great network of fortified towns over his kingdom. Leofham was to play its part in the strategy and we were to help build and maintain a bridge over the river Leof. The king's chief mason would be arriving shortly to plan the work. A charter was also being prepared which would grant Thane Pelhere rights to the forest land across the river. This was a mark of the king's special favour and the thane was deeply honoured. A road was planned too which would link Leofham with other fortified towns beyond us.

For several days the king and his retinue remained in Leofham but no word reached Morcant and me about any royal decision concerning us. The thane was completely occupied with entertaining them and I settled determinedly in my workshop to finish my private project with that baulk of timber. Swefred could not do much but at least he managed to protect me from visitors.

"I want to make this before I get sent off with the fyrdmen," I explained, not wishing to consider any other even less pleasant alternatives. "Then if I don't come back at least I will have made something interesting!"

The day came for the charter to be sealed and witnessed and Morcant and I had still heard nothing. A great table was set up outside in front of the hall for the king. The thane's henchmen stood by and as many of the rest of Leofham's population as could be squeezed into the area with any hope of seeing anything at all gathered at a respectful distance to watch. At a signal from a royal trumpeter, each of the king's attendant earldormen came forward with dignified ceremony to witness the charter. The king spoke a few words to Thane Pelhere who knelt before him. In my mind's eye I could see our descendants clearing the forest and growing more crops in its fertile soil, just as our forebears had done. Now we did not have the strength but it would come. When we had peace from the Vikings we would be able to turn our attention to the land. We would ...

Morcant nudged me. "Wulfgar," he whispered, "do you know what one of the charter provisions is?"

I shook my head.

"No dragon is to be slain throughout the land granted to the thane, unless the creature harms people or livestock."

At the end of the ceremony there was much cheering from the villagers and the thane presented the king with the cup I had turned and engraved with the dragons and Hund. I was not able to hear much from my position in the crowd but I could see the King examining the cup carefully and and talking animatedly to the thane. I could tell he liked it and I was pleased. I slipped back to the workshop and settled down to putting the finishing touches to my private project.

I had just swept the last of the shavings from the floor in readiness for supper when a lad trotted into the workshop with the unwelcome message I had been expecting.

"Thane Pelhere wants to see you at noon tomorrow ... Wow! did it really have a head like that?"

"Yes it did," I replied irritably, "now go home!"

"Wow! Did you make it?"

"Yes! Now go home!"

"Wow!"

Chapter 13
Banished

I did not sleep well that night and when I did drift off, it was into a very troubled slumber. At first light there was a hammering on the workshop door. I staggered to open it: the lad who had been the messenger of the night before was shivering in the gloom outside.

"What do you want?" I asked in some surprise.

"You've to bring it with you."

"What?" I was scarcely awake.

"That dragon thing. You've to bring it. Thane's orders," and he was gone.

"What is it all about?" I asked Morcant later when I had had time to wake up properly and had gone across to his hut.

He shrugged his shoulders, "I can't say," he replied, "but I think it is a good sign."

Morcant and I were punctual at the hall. Royal guards had been posted at the door and we were escorted forward to the dais by soldiers who left us in no doubt that we were under formal arrest and who showed no interest in the weird lump of timber tucked under my arm except to order me to leave it by the door.

The king, seated under the dragon-bone arch with Thane Pelhere and Earldorman Æthelnoth standing by, barely acknowledged us as we knelt before him. It was a long time before he spoke.

"This is a sad business, Morcant of Tyddewi. You have allowed your desire for scholarship to lead you into the sin of disloyalty. I had thought to promote you to great things in Wessex. Someone of your accomplishments would have guided well such an abbey as I wish to found at Shaftesbury. Canterbury itself would have been within your grasp. Pope John himself seeks scholars such as you in Rome. But no high office in Wessex can ever be yours now. My sentence is that you will remain here in Leofham until the day of your death."

Morcant lifted his head slightly and met the king's eyes. There was the very slightest flicker that showed that the two men understood each other perfectly and then it was gone as if a mask had been drawn across the king's face.

"You may go," he said quietly. "Go and pray ever for your king."

"Thank you, my dear liege lord, from the bottom of my heart," murmured Morcant and as the king transferred his gaze to me he slipped away.

There was a long pause. Under the king's piecing gaze I bowed my head further forward until I could see nothing but the hall floor. Silence.

"And you, Wulfgar Waelwulfson," said the king, just as I was wondering if anyone was ever going to speak again, "you have joined in disobedience to my loyal thane. You have no scholarship to excuse *you*. What talent have you?"

"None, my liege," I stammered, "that is ... that is ... none, my liege."

The thane must have lent across to the king because they exchanged some words. Then a henchman strode past me towards the back of the hall. There was a pause and his boots passed my bent form on their way back. A slight murmur from the king and then another very long silence.

Then suddenly the king was speaking, "I find, Wulfgar Waelwulfson, that not only are you disobedient, you are not quite truthful. I will ask you again. What talent have you been given by the Almighty God?"

"My liege," I was stammering again, "I don't ... that is ... I am a carpenter, my liege ... and I carve wood a little ..."

"Look at me, Wulfgar Waelwulfson!" commanded the king and I raised my eyes to meet his. They were kind eyes, I found myself thinking, although they were set in a face as stern as steel and unbending as rock. "For your part in this disobedience I sentence you, Wulfgar Waelwulfson, Woodcarver, to a period of banishment from my dear realm of Wessex. You will leave for France before the next moon. I will ensure that Master Morcant has all the directions you need. You may go."

Chapter 14
But Not Banished

"But I don't understand!" I said. "What are you so pleased about? I'm banished for however long the king sees fit – that could be the rest of my life! It's alright for you – you never wanted to be anywhere except Leofham anyway and as for rising in church office as far as Rome, the very idea would make you shudder but I don't want ..."

Morcant held up his hand, "You are right, Wulfgar, all believers are equal in God's sight and I am grateful to the king for removing me from the temptation to seek what the church now calls 'high office'. But don't you see what the king is doing for you? He liked the cup you made for him, and he told the thane he thought you had some useful skill but then, I hear, he was taken aback by the beauty of the carving of the dragon's head! He wants to help you, Wulfgar. He has given me what I most need and desire under the guise of punishment and he's done the same for you too!"

"What!" I was astounded, "I'm sorry, Morcant, but how can banishment be what I need?"

"Sit down," said Morcant, "and listen to me. You are a talented carver of wood. That much is clear now that you have shown what you can do. But you are untaught. The king is sending you to be trained by the best Frankish master craftsmen. Earldorman Æthelnoth has handed me these royal letters here which are addressed to the clerk of the building work which is going on at the Abbey of Corvey in Francia. You are to work with his master craftsmen at Corvey until you have learned everything they can teach you. Then you are to return to Wessex where you will be able to use your talents in the service of your king who is eager to have skilled master craftsmen here in Wessex for his building projects."

I still could not take it in, "What?" I said again stupidly, "what do you mean, Morcant?"

"You will leave Leofham with the royal party and will sail for France under the charge of some monks who are scribes the king is sending to Corvey to study in Abbot Bovo's new scriptorium there. The Abbot will arrange for your return in due course."

The great black cloud lifted. I was not really banished at all! I was being sent abroad to learn my craft and when I had learnt I would simply come home again. Those kind eyes in that stern face! I remembered them twinkling at me – as though the king would let me know I was to come to no harm.

"God be praised!" I cried, "and long live our King Alfred of Wessex!"

Glossary and Notes

Here are some words you might not have met before:

Church scot   a tax paid to church officials often in grain. This is the origin of the phrase "scot-free".

Ealdorman   a royal official of high rank, usually in charge of one or more shires.

Fyrd   an army based originally on men who would return home after a short term of duty.

Palfrey   a riding horse specially suitable for long journeys.

Royal Vill   The king had a number of residences, called Vills, which acted as administrative centres throughout Wessex. He moved round these rather than remaining in one place. This enabled him to keep contact with the whole of his kingdom and also prevented any one area from being solely responsible for providing food etc. for the king and his retainers.

Shire moot   a court that maintained local order.

Thane   (sometimes spelled thegn) a nobleman below the rank of Ealdorman.

Some of you might be wondering about the dragon which Wulfgar and his friends encountered in this story. Fossils of a modestly sized sauropod dinosaur were discovered in 1983 and named *Shunosaurus*. It is estimated to have been almost 10 metres long from head to tail and to have stood well over 3 metres tall. At the end of its tail was a spiked club capable of dealing a crushing blow to a theropod dinosaur, should it be attacked by one. On the tomb of Bishop Bell in Carlisle Cathedral, which dates from 1496, there is a clear depiction of two such animals. The other dragon in the story is a theropod of some kind, perhaps like the one which seems to be mentioned in the epic poem *Beowulf* c.1000.

Wulfgar and the Dragon

Wulfgar and the Dragon

Wulfgar and the Dragon

Wulfgar and the Dragon

Wulfgar and the Dragon

Wulfgar and the Dragon

Wulfgar and the Dragon

Wulfgar and the Dragon

Wulfgar and the Dragon